# LOST FOR WORDS

## ILLUSTRATED CROSSWORD CLUES
## FOR ADDICTS AND AMATEURS

## JON RILEY AND OZYMANDIAS

ANGUS
& ROBERTSON
PUBLISHERS

# How to use this book

*Lost For Words* contains the illustrated clues to two complete crosswords: the clues (*across* and then *down*) are contained within the book.

Answers can be filled in on the grids on the inside of the back cover and the solutions can be found on the last page of the book.

*ANGUS & ROBERTSON PUBLISHERS*

*16 Golden Square, London W1R 4BN,*
*United Kingdom,*
*and Unit 4, Eden Park, 31 Waterloo Road,*
*North Ryde, NSW, Australia 2113*

*First published in the United Kingdom by*
*Angus & Robertson (UK) in 1988*
*First published in Australia by*
*Angus & Robertson Publishers in 1988*

*Copyright © Litterarti Ltd 1988*
*A Litterarti/Running Heads Book*

*British Library Cataloguing in Publication Data*
*Riley, Jon*
    *Lost for words : illustrated crossword*
    *clues for addicts and amateurs.*
    *1. Crossword puzzles*
    *I. Title   II. Ozymandias*
    *793.73'2*

*ISBN 0 207 16002 3*

*Typeset in Great Britain by New Faces, Bedford*
*Printed in Great Britain by Hazell Watson & Viney Ltd*

**FOREWORD**

A dusty train crawls through the Egyptian landscape. In a first-class compartment a man sits scribbling in a battered notebook. Suddenly he looks up at his fellow travellers and announces, 'Hit lass kinkily with a bit of a smack.' The other passengers stare politely out of the window. As he looks down again someone slips him a scrap of paper with the word 'Saltish' written under a small drawing.

The traveller looks up. 'Discharge of a fly spray?' he ventures. Nobody stirs. The aristocratic-looking woman in the corner reads her novel, a young couple continue to stare into each other's eyes, a fat man delicately peels a peach. Puzzled, the traveller puts the drawing in his pocket. 'Bear and crocodile in cahoots,' he murmurs. Before he can look up another drawing has found its way onto his pad. He glances quickly at the young man in the corner – didn't he have a pen in his hand?

The train pulls into the hot and busy station, the vendors crowd up to the windows, selling luke-warm drinks and sweetmeats. As the fat man squeezes himself through the door he knocks over a canvas bag and out tumble dozens of sheets of paper. The floor is strewn with drawings. The young man desperately tries to gather them up. The traveller bends down to help him: 'Falling out? Bra holds this' he says. 'Bust-up,' comes the reply.

So met the crossword compiler and the cartoonist – Ozymandias and Jon Riley. A cryptic meeting in Egypt.

# CROSSWORD No.1

**1** Across: Strange form of life meeting big town girl (happy event) (8)

**5** Across: Party with wobbly bust is hesitant (6)

**10** Across: 'Bend over!' Highwayman's demand to get twice as much bread (6,4,5)

*? Double your dough?*

**11** Across: Gypsy with cane belaboured love (7)

Romance

**12** Across: Content of capsule, maybe, baffle
holding one quiet (4–3)

**13** Across: Fine shot by Jacques? It's big fellow that croaks (8)

**15** Across: Hose buffets (5)

**18** Across: Gardener's enemy, one with swaying hips (5)

**20** Across: Imaginative use of language causing
wayward poet harm (8)

*metaphor*

**23** Across: One boozin' swallows last of bitter poison (7)

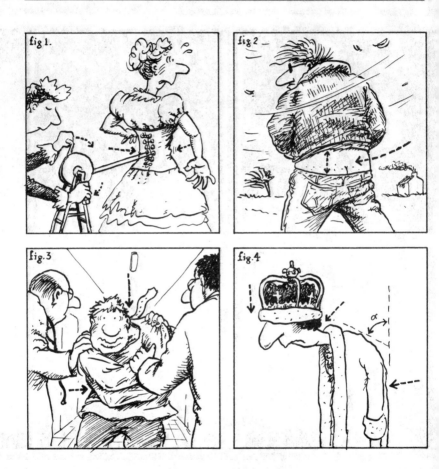

**25** Across: Clothing that contributes to back-ache misery (7)

**26** Across: Top dog, perhaps, each leg embellished
with soft knit (4,2,3,6)

**27** Across: Unquestioning followers head for sun in land of Arabs (3-3)

**28** Across: Nonsensical chorus – sheep learning backing (8)

**1** Down: Hat was nourishing before one (6)

**2** Down: High output speaker making mud-hut loo vibrate (9)

**3** Down: Regimental bigwig, solitary, in mountain pass (7)

*colonel*

**4** Down: Bit of stuffing involved in unhealthy meals (5)

*thyme?*

**6** Down: Duck on shifting moss is showing
tendency to seep through (7)

**7** Down: Gambler's house, place for lunatics to die (5)

**8** Down: Nomad almost swept up girl – it conjures visions of far away (8)

# CROSSWORD No.1

**9** Down: Sort of feast – odd way of having fun in bay (8)

**14** Down: Train emu with difficulty to imitate
cow? (8)

**16** Down: One warbling in Church: 'To err is misguided' (9)

**17** Down: Hanky-panky created by cheeky opener of doors (8)

**19** Down: Fancy drink with model (7)

**21** Down: Horse, mixed type, with no use for comb (7)

**22** Down: Show about meat (6)

**24** Down: Mysterious characters given treatment by nurse (5)

**25** Down: Statement of conviction convict's beginning to go over again (5)

# CROSSWORD No.2

**1** Across: Piano playing preacher's Lenin – it gives writers tips (6-9)

**9** Across: Bit part a little weak in playing role (5)

**10** Across: Exotic soup ingredient sends Brit crazy (5-4)

**11** Across: Dirty books? Censor brought in hit hard at ultimate in pornography (9)

**12** Across: Needles stuck in nasty liquid (5)

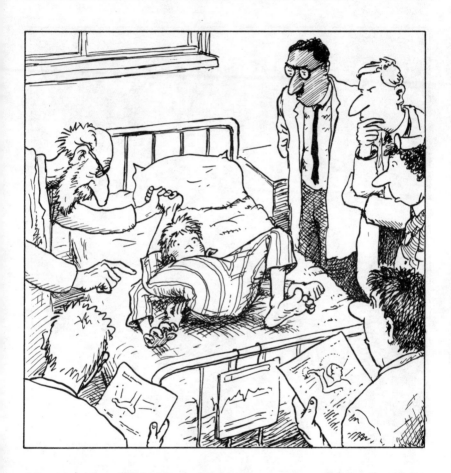

**13** Across: Old doctor twisting part of foot back round child's head (5)

**15** Across: Car going berserk in crowds kills a lot (9)

MASSACRES

## CROSSWORD No.2

**18** Across: Nasty smell in change of climate (changing chemically) (9)

**19** Across: To produce litter there's fresh charge
(3-2)

**21** Across: Is mum supplying rumour? (3-2)

**23** Across: Bankrupt fairy appearing in interval (9)

**25** Across: Composer, wildly artistical, cutting one in Rome (9)

## LOST FOR WORDS

**26** Across: What cows do is bark! (5)

**27** Across: It tends to get snarled up with fish
chaps caught – unsnarling required (15)

**1** Down: Mate holding oars awkwardly –
protection from sun required (7)

# CROSSWORD No.2

**2** Down: Where you'd find daily, topless one was dancing with man (9)

## LOST FOR WORDS

**3** Down: Chilly dwelling, one with endless dreariness (5)

**4** Down: Snob mural, lambasted as 'below par'
(9)

**5** Down: One diminutive bishop always in dress (5)

**CROSSWORD No.2**

**6** Down: Offensive outburst: it may cause delay
in driving off (4-5)

**7** Down: Strapped man's rear eyed in kinky fashion (5)

**8** Down: Keeps slurping retsina? (7)

RETAINS

**14** Down: Awful apparition: tramp holding head of giraffe, sightless, tailless (9)

**16** Down: Shutting out what's mostly reverse of melodious in chant (9)

**17** Down: Agent left in charge consumed copy (9)

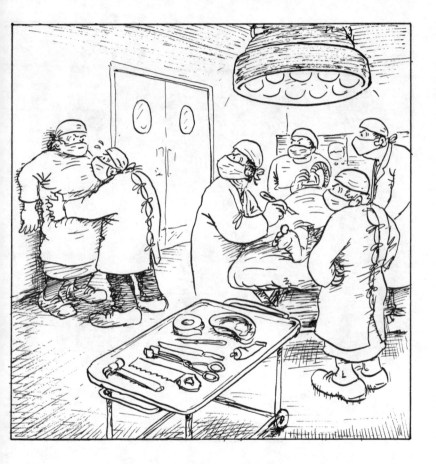

**18** Down: Molested, as Susie is in doctor's clutches (7)

**20** Down: Hamper shut up with short vicar in (7)

**22** Down: Age certainly holds painter up (5)

**23** Down: Bread cheers when you've put stone on (5)

**24** Down: Bible supporter well below par (5)

# SOLUTIONS

## CROSSWORD No.1

ACROSS: 1) Felicity 5) Doubts 10) Double your money 11) Romance 12) Fish-oil 13) Bullfrog 15) Socks 18) Aphis 20) Metaphor 23) Atropin 25) Chemise 26) King of the castle 27) Yes-men 28) Folderol

DOWN: 1) Fedora 2) Loudmouth 3) Colonel 4) Thyme 6) Osmosis 7) Bingo 8) Spyglass 9) Bunfight 14) Ruminate 16) Chorister 17) Malarkey 19) Suppose 21) Piebald 22) Reveal 24) Runes 25) Credo

## CROSSWORD No.2

ACROSS: 1) Pencil-sharpener 9) Rowel 10) Birds-nest 11) Scatology 12) Styli 13) Leech 15) Massacres 18) Metabolic 19) Top-up 21) Say-so 23) Pauperise 25) Scarlatti 26) Graze 27) Disentanglement

DOWN: 1) Parasol 2) Newsagent 3) Igloo 4) Subnormal 5) Array 6) Push-start 7) Needy 8) Retains 14) Hobgoblin 16) Secluding 17) Replicate 18) Misused 20) Prevent 22) Years 23) Pitta 24) Eagle